WARRIOR HEROES

THE PHARAOH'S CHARIOTEER

BENJAMIN HULME-CROSS

Illustrated by

Angelo Rinaldi

BLOOMSBURY EDUCATION
AN IMPRINT OF BLOOMSBURY

LONDON OXFORD NEW YORK NEW DELHI SYDNEY

CONTENTS

INTRODUCTION
THE HALL OF HEROES

The Hall of Heroes is a museum
all about warriors throughout
history. It's full of swords, bows
and arrows, helmets, boats, armour,
shields, spears, axes and just
about anything else that a warrior
might need. But this isn't just
another museum full of old stuff
in glass cases - it's also haunted
by the ghosts of the warriors whose
belongings are there.

Our great grandfather, Professor
Blade, set up the museum and when
he died he started haunting the
place too. He felt guilty about the
trapped ghost warriors and vowed he
would not rest in peace until all
the other ghosts were laid to rest
first. And that's where Arthur and
I come in...

On the night of the Professor's funeral Arthur and I broke into the museum - we knew it was wrong but we just couldn't help ourselves. And that's when we discovered something very weird. When we are touched by one of the ghost warriors we get transported to the time and place where the ghost lived and died. And we can't get back until we've fixed whatever it is that keeps the ghost from resting in peace. So we go from one mission to the next, recovering lost swords, avenging deaths, saving loved ones or doing whatever else the ghost warrior needs us to do.

Fortunately while the Professor was alive I wrote down everything he ever told us about these warriors in a book I call *Warrior Heroes* - so luckily we do have some idea of what we're getting into each time - even if Arthur does still call me 'Finn the geek'. But we need more than a book to survive each adventure because wherever we go we're surrounded by war and battle and the fiercest fighters who ever lived, as you're about to find out!

CHAPTER 1

"We're going to Egypt!" Finn yelped. He adored his great grandfather, Professor Blade, and hoped to follow in his footsteps as an archaeologist. Nowhere suggested the adventure of exploring history quite like Egypt.

"I do believe so," replied the Professor's ghost, leaning back in his chair and removing his glasses to clean them with a handkerchief.

"Not really warriors though, were they?" Arthur remarked. "Isn't Egypt all about pyramids and pharaohs and mummies?"

"Oh, they did their fair share of fighting," the Professor assured him. "You don't establish a civilisation that lasts for three thousand years without waging a few wars!" Finn's ears pricked up as the Professor began telling them about Nubian fortresses in the land to the south, Hittites attacking from the north, and sea raiders sailing into the Nile Delta from the Mediterranean.

"The thing about the Egyptians was that they were lucky enough to live in an incredibly fertile land that allowed them to grow far more food than they needed." Arthur began to glaze over at this point, although Finn still listened closely. "So they had spare time to fight wars and build temples and pyramids. We know a lot about them because they left so much behind for us to find."

"And what about our next ghost?" Arthur wondered out loud, bored by the history lesson.

"Something of a mystery, this chap," said the Professor, leaning towards his desk enthusiastically. "We think he may have been a nobleman or a lesser prince because of how he was buried. He was young when he died – only about sixteen or seventeen. And it was a violent death. We could see that when we examined the mummy."

"Hang on a minute," said Finn. "I think we're about to find out!" Sure enough, the air in the Professor's study seemed to grow colder, and it felt charged with something like static electricity.

The boys shivered in anticipation as they heard light footsteps approaching along the corridor. No matter how often it happened, they were always awestruck when they met one of the ghost-warriors.

The lights in the study dimmed and then disappeared altogether as the electricity cut out. The Professor and the boys made their way carefully over to the fireplace, where they could see a little in the flickering firelight. Across the room, the door creaked slowly open, and in walked a young Egyptian man, instantly recognisable by his striped headdress, chunky gold necklace and white kilt. He looked around the room curiously, and seeing the group huddled by the fire, he walked towards them. As the young man drew nearer, the boys were both struck by his eyes,

thickly defined by black eyeliner and decorated with green paint so that it looked almost as if each eye were at the centre of a green leaf.

"I am Thamose," the Egyptian said in a weak voice.

"And what service might we be able to provide you with, sir?" the Professor asked gently. "How is it that your soul still walks the earth, unable to rest?"

"The first part of my father's reign was marked by peace and prosperity," Thamose began slowly. "Then something happened that changed everything. War broke out between my father's army and the Nubians."

"So you were... are the pharaoh's son?" Finn asked, eyes wide.

"My father was Pharaoh, yes. But my mother

was Nubian. So when the two kingdoms were at war... Well, things became very difficult for my mother, and thousands of other mothers besides."

"And you died in this war?" the Professor enquired.

"Worse... Far worse... I was taken hostage by the Nubians before the war began. They hoped to force my father to pay them tribute. They did not think he would raise an army. You see," he said, finally looking each of them in the eye, "it was always my desire to honour my father by fighting bravely as one of his charioteers. I never thought I would be the reason a war started. I was the reason my mother's life ended the way it did. I was the reason thousands of Nubians and thousands of Egyptians died."

Finn and Arthur looked at one another. This sounded like a most unusual mission.

"So you need us to...?" Finn left the question hanging.

"Go to Thebes and prevent the war from happening!" said Thamose. "Save thousands of lives!" He was standing directly in front of the boys now, and reached out a hand to grasp each by the arm. It wasn't a sensation they would ever get used to. The room began to spin and the firelight turned into a belt of light accelerating around them, until it vanished completely.

CHAPTER 2

F inn woke with a jolt, unable to see, kicking out sharply with both legs. His foot connected with something hard. There was a loud crash and then a rhythmic scraping sound as if something were spinning to the floor in the darkness. It always took a few minutes for the boys to remember where they were supposed to be when they first woke up in a new time, and this was no exception. Finn gulped down the panic that threatened to overwhelm him, alone in the dark.

He listened closely as the scraping sound stopped, but it seemed that nobody had been disturbed. So, feeling carefully to check for any more noisy objects, he stood up. He now discovered it was not as dark as he had at first believed. In one direction he could see a small window through which the moon cast a little pale light. The moonbeams acted like a spotlight, and although everything else remained in shadow one thing was lit up beautifully.

"A chariot!" Finn whispered, as something dawned on him. He stooped down and patted around on the floor to find the object he had kicked over. Sure enough his fingers found the edge of a wheel lying flat on the earthen floor. Stepping carefully around the wheel, Finn made his way towards the chariot. It was like a small cart, with a low, open-backed platform on two wheels and a waist-high guard wall that curved around three sides. Carved into the metal guard was a selection of human figures with animal heads, shown side-on.

Finn recognised the carved figures from objects he'd seen in the Hall of Heroes. *I'm in Egypt*, he thought. And this must be a chariot workshop.

The details of why he was there came flooding back. *The Professor! The pharaoh! The Nubians kidnapping Thamose! I have to find Arthur!*

Finn moved cautiously over to the window and traced his way along the wall, sliding his palms along its smooth, dry surface until they found a door. He stepped out into a quiet street and waited for his senses to adjust.

The air was very warm and dry, and a gentle breeze carried on it the faint smell of a herb or spice that Finn did not recognise. The moon shone down on simple but well-built buildings that seemed to be coated in something smooth, a bit like cement. The street was narrow and empty, and in one direction Finn could see light shimmering on water. He headed towards it and soon emerged onto a busier street. All around him now were the sounds of laughter and chatter. The road ran parallel to a wide river, presumably the Nile, and on the opposite bank Finn could see the great stone walls, temples and palaces that you might expect to find in an ancient Egyptian city.

This must be Thebes, Finn thought. *And that must be where the pharaoh lives!* He stood and stared across the river until the thought of Arthur wrenched him away. One of the brothers usually found that they woke up in the middle of a very dangerous situation, and seeing as Finn's introduction to Egypt had been relatively gentle, he could only assume that Arthur was in trouble somewhere nearby. He began wandering along the road by the river and was surprised to find it lined with taverns. Somehow he hadn't imagined that taverns existed in ancient Egypt. When he drew level with a particularly rowdy tavern he strolled inside and began looking for his brother.

He was distracted almost immediately by a group of twenty or so men and women who were huddled around a table. Most had the same striking eye paint that Thamose's ghost had worn. Pushing his way to the front of this group, he found a mixed-race teenage girl and an Egyptian man playing a board game. Finn watched, fascinated, as the man picked up four painted sticks and threw them on the table, drawing groans from the crowd, and then swore and moved one of the counters on the board. Finn noticed a dagger and a necklace lying on the table beside the board. It looked as though the players were gambling. The girl reached for the sticks and Finn was about to move on when he saw, out of the corner of his eye, that the girl made a very strange motion with her wrist. She threw her sticks down and this time the crowd roared their approval. She moved all of her tokens off the board and stood up, reaching for the dagger and the necklace.

As she did so, another coloured stick fell from her hand and clattered down to join the others on the table. There were gasps from the crowd and her opponent's face darkened.

"You've cheated!" he shouted, slamming his fist down on the table.

The girl snatched up the gold-handled dagger and whipped it from its sheath. Finn glanced around the table. Several of the men looked very angry. Acting on the sort of impulse that sometimes overtook his naturally cautious calculations, Finn grabbed the girl's hand.

"Come on!" he shouted. "Run!"

The girl needed no encouragement. They dashed out of the tavern together and tore off along the road beside the river. Almost immediately Finn realised he was no use to the girl at all.

"Where are we running?" the girl panted, her eyes wide and bright. Finn glanced at her as they ran and had the unsettling sense that she was more excited by this experience than afraid. But of course her question had laid bare the problem. Finn knew nothing about Thebes. He had no idea whether the girl had committed a terrible crime or whether the man and his friends were likely to pursue them. And he had no idea where to hide.

Behind them they heard angry shouts.

"Follow me!" the girl said, sensing his indecision. She veered off the main road and up a modest street similar to the one where the chariot workshop had been. Then she darted into a narrow alleyway and sped along it.

Finn struggled to keep up with her. The gap between them widened, until he followed her around a corner and found... nothing.

The girl had disappeared! Finn emerged into a small courtyard with three alleyways running off it in different directions. But before he could begin to think about which route to take he felt cold metal at his throat.

"Who are you, boy?" the girl hissed in his ear. "You don't seem to know Thebes at all!"

"I'm nobody," Finn said, praying the deflection would work. "I'm new to town but I wanted to help because those men looked pretty angry." It was always difficult to find a satisfactory lie about who he was and where he came from when he arrived in a new time, and he hated doing it.

"I find it very suspicious," the girl said, "that

you, a stranger to Thebes, just walked into a tavern and the first person you spoke to was me."

This seemed an odd thing to say. What was so special about this girl: a gambler and a cheat and probably a thief?

"What do you mean? Who are you?" Finn asked, hoping to move the subject away from himself.

"Good question," came a gruff, angry voice. "Who is the little viper?" Finn's heart surged with relief at the sound. A paranoid thief holding a knife to his throat was a terrible start to the mission, and he was angry with the girl for being so ungrateful. All he wanted was to slip away and find Arthur.

"They're arguing now but they were in it together," someone else said. "Let's make sure they never steal again."

The girl let go of Finn and both of them spun around. Finn's heart sank. Inevitably it was a group of men from the tavern who had found them. There were four of them, fanned out across the courtyard. They each held vicious-looking curved swords like scythes and standing a little in front of the others was the man who had been playing the game. Judging by their expressions and the way they held their swords, the men's intentions were lethal!

* * *

Arthur floated contentedly in the water, gazing up at a velvety night sky scattered with a million diamond stars. He had no idea where he was and he was perfectly relaxed, as if he had just woken up from a very long, deep sleep. His blank mind registered the sound of a paddle pulling through water. *Must be a boat nearby,* Arthur thought lazily. And then the paddle connected with his head.

He recoiled from the blow, crying out and submerging his face at the same time. Water filled his mouth, his head rang and the rest of his body jolted into action, thrashing in wild panic as he realised he was under water. He came up gasping for air and shouting for help. A small rowing boat lay alongside him and he grabbed at its side.

"Give me your hand, friend," someone said, and a few seconds later Arthur had been hauled out of the water and lay sprawled in the bottom of the boat. His rescuer, a teenage boy of mixed race, was the boat's only other occupant, and Arthur thanked him, wiping the water from his eyes.

"Where am I?" he asked, rubbing a very tender bruise on the side of his head.

"That blow from the oar must have addled your senses! You are on the River Nile of course. But how did you come to be here, swimming at night? Do you not fear the crocodiles?"

Arthur looked up and shook his head slowly, trying to buy time as the memories crowded in: *Egypt – the Professor – Finn!*

"Can you take me to Thebes?" he asked. The boy laughed.

"Of course! Thebes is behind us and Thebes is in front of us. I'm going to the east side, if that's alright with you. You can call me Thami."

Thamose! Arthur thought with a flash of recognition. He nodded and thanked Thami again as the boy began to paddle. Picking up a spare paddle, Arthur joined in.

"I'm Arthur," he said as they moved across the calm water. "I'm here to find my brother." This didn't really explain why he was floating in the river, but Arthur figured he would be able to blame his head injury for any gaps in his story.

"And I need to find my sister," said Thami. "Perhaps we can help each other."

They were close to the shore now, close

enough to hear the raised voices coming from the taverns as the people of Thebes drank and made merry. They heard angry shouts, and saw a group of men pointing along the riverbank at two fleeing figures.

"That's my sister!" shouted Thami, just as Arthur yelled, "That's my brother!"

They pulled frantically with their paddles, desperate to reach land as the men chased after Thami's sister and Finn. At the side of the river Thami hastily tied the boat to a wooden post and reached down to grab a fishing net. He threw a boat hook to Arthur before leaping out and racing up the bank. They were just in time to see the last of the men disappearing down a narrow side street and they followed in hot pursuit, soon entering the alleyway that Finn had run down a few moments earlier.

They rushed towards the courtyard and saw the men all standing around. Without breaking stride, Thami hurled the net at the group. Two of the men went down, cursing in the tangle. Thami's sister lunged at the man she had conned and he stepped back just as Arthur swung the boathook through the air and knocked him out with a blow to the head. Finn leapt forward and grabbed the unconscious man's sword before he, Arthur and the girl turned and began to advance on the one remaining man. He took a few moments to calculate the odds, then turned and ran.

"Nefi, what have you done this time?" said Thami to his sister. "More gambling I suppose?"

"Oh, brother, you sound like the high priest,"

Nefi flashed back, pulling a face. Then, looking at Finn, she said, "Thank you, stranger. I apologise for the trap. I am in your debt."

EXTRACT FROM *WARRIOR HEROES*
BY FINN BLADE

THE RIVER NILE

Egypt was the first real nation in the world, and the first great civilisation, and nearly everything for which Egypt is famous was possible because the largest river in the world flowed through the country.

In a land that saw virtually no rain, the Nile was the source of all life. Every year, far away near the source of the river, there were heavy rains and melting snow that swelled the Nile and caused it to burst its banks by the time it reached Egypt. The resulting flood spread rich silt all over the land around the river. Once the water subsided, the fields it left behind were perfect for growing crops. So the Nile provided Egypt with nearly all her:

- food: the main food crop was wheat, used to make much more bread than everyone needed. Of course the river was also a source of fish and water birds.

- drink: the Egyptians also grew a lot of barley, which they used to make beer.

- clothes: flax was grown and from it the Egyptians made linen, which they traded and used to make clothes.

- papyrus: reeds grown in the Nile could be used to make papyrus, the first sort of paper in the world.

- transport: the river was the perfect way to move people and materials around the kingdom.

CHAPTER 3

"We should tell them, sister. They have helped us and we have helped them, and we are bonded by it."

Nefi held up her hand and looked intently into Arthur's eyes, tipping her head to one side, and then repeated the exercise with Finn. They were all in Thami's boat in the middle of the river, drifting slowly on the lazy current.

They could no longer hear the voices from the riverbank and it felt as if they were completely alone. Finally Nefi nodded.

"I am not a thief," she said abruptly. "I am Princess Nefru and this is my brother, Prince Thamose." Arthur and Finn exchanged a relieved glance. Fate had a way of throwing them into the path of whoever they needed to meet when they began a new mission, but in the rush of the action neither of them had been completely certain that Thami was in fact Thamose.

"So your father is... the pharaoh?" Finn asked, feigning more wide-eyed surprise than he felt. Thami nodded.

"And our mother is the Nubian queen, which is why we do not look like other princes and princesses of Egypt," he said, running a hand over his dark-skinned cheek and smiling.

Arthur and Thami began paddling again, and as they made their leisurely way across the Nile, Nefi and Thami took turns explaining that they felt trapped in the palace and that they often escaped to roam the streets of Thebes on the other side of the river at night.

"The problem is that my sister likes to make these little excursions alone, keeping them a secret even from me, and then I have to come after her and find her, as I did tonight, to extract her from the trouble she creates!" Thami looked back over his shoulder at Nefi, frowning, but she just laughed and splashed water at him.

"And what of you two?" Nefi asked. "What has brought you to Thebes?"

"Our father is a merchant from a country far from here," said Finn quickly. He'd been preparing his story. "We came with him and he abandoned us here." He hated lying, but they had to be from somewhere, and the twenty-first century wasn't much of an answer!

"Well, for now you shall be our guests at the palace," said Thami. "You must allow us to thank you for helping us."

* * *

Arthur awoke the next morning to the distant sound of a screeching heron. He and Finn had spent the night in Thami's rooms. When the prince tried to offer them his bed it turned out that everyone was equally stubborn, and nobody was willing to sleep on a bed while the others slept on rush mats on the floor. So they had all slept on the floor.

Arthur looked around the cool, dark room and found that he was alone. Laid out at one end of his mat was a pile of new clothes. He noticed his own and Finn's clothes in a second pile and concluded the new clothes were for him. The light tunic slipped over his head easily enough, but figuring out how to wear the kilt that he had seen worn by all the Egyptian men the night before took more effort. After several attempts he managed to fasten it around his waist and after strapping on some sandals he walked out of Thami's room, feeling rather self-conscious.

The next room was brighter, and led out onto a balcony. The heat hit him as if he'd just opened an oven door and he squinted against the bright sunlight, taking a few moments to adjust to his new environment. He found himself looking across a huge public square. Along one side of the square stood what had to be a temple, its vast doorway marked on either side by painted statues as tall as lamp posts. Animal-headed humans, they made for fearsome guards. Arthur suddenly felt very small. He was used to feeling out of his depth during his and Finn's adventures but here, in ancient Egypt, he was well over three thousand years away from home. Everything felt very, very alien.

"The palace temple of Amen," said Thami, appearing at Arthur's side. "There is a bigger one on the other side of the river. My grandfather built this one. It's beautiful, no?" Arthur swallowed and nodded.

"Look!" Thami pointed at two small figures crossing the square towards the temple doors. It took Arthur a few moments to recognise his brother, now in Egyptian dress, accompanying Nefi to the temple. He was slightly annoyed that they had all left him to sleep, and was about to suggest that he and Thami joined them, when there was a cough behind him.

"The queen wishes to speak with you, my prince." The man who had appeared on the balcony carried a long spear in one hand, and from his belt hung the same sort of curved, scythe-like sword that Arthur had seen the previous night. But more than anything else Arthur's eyes were drawn to the bright gold sun emblazoned on the man's white tunic.

"He is a temple guard," said Thami. "Half

monk and half soldier. My mother the queen says that these are the most dangerous of men, and we are fortunate to have them guarding us." The guard's face was an expressionless mask and Arthur found him deeply unnerving.

"Come," said Thami. "Let's go." He led Arthur back inside and through the dark inner corridors of the building. Arthur was not sure he wanted to meet the queen, who might well have concerns about her children picking up foreigners in the alleyways of Thebes. But he kept his worries to himself and followed close behind Thami. At one point he looked over his shoulder at the guard who walked behind them. For the briefest moment, Arthur saw something in the man's face change. Looking straight ahead as he walked, he wore the same emotionless stare as he had on the balcony. But before that the guard's eyes had been filled with hate. Arthur did not know what to make of it, but one thing he was completely sure of. The temple guard was no friend.

All such thoughts were expelled from his mind when Thami led him past two more temple guards and into a large, lavish room. The walls and floor were covered with hangings and rugs. The tables glinted with the gold and polished stone trinkets

they were littered with. And in the middle of it all there stood the queen, her glittering green robes embroidered with gold. Everything about her was striking, from her clothes to her physical beauty, but most astonishing of all was her gaze, which when directed at Arthur forced him to stare at the floor, dry-mouthed and lost for words.

Thami laughed and patted him on the back. "He has a very good heart, Mother. Tell the guards to leave and I will tell you how I met him."

"Come to me, boy," said the queen, and Arthur shuffled forward. She cupped his chin in her hand and brought his head up slowly until they were eye to eye. She angled her head slightly as she did this, just as Nefi had in the boat, and held his gaze for a while before smiling and letting him go.

"Very well," she said, waving the temple guards

out of the room. "Tell me your story." Thami proceeded to tell his mother everything that had taken place the previous evening. Arthur was stunned. Weren't these night-time adventures on the streets in Thebes supposed to be secret? From the way Thami spoke it was clear that the queen was familiar with her children's habits and watching her reactions to Thami's story it seemed to Arthur that she approved of what they did.

"So my son saved your life," said the queen when Thami had finished. "But you and your brother helped save Nefi's life. It appears I am in your debt."

Arthur's face betrayed his total confusion, and the queen looked at him very seriously.

"I encourage Thamose and Nefru to leave the

palace as often as possible. They must learn to survive. I am pleased that they have made two friends whom they can trust. The gods know my children have enough enemies..."

"Mother!" Thami hissed, nodding towards the closed door and placing a finger over his lips. In hushed tones, the queen explained that she was not the main queen; she was one of the pharaoh's secondary wives. "The palace is full of plotting between the queens, all of whom secretly hope that a son of theirs will be Pharaoh one day. All I want is for Thami and Nefi to make it out of the palace grown up and alive!"

* * *

Finn gazed in awe at the painted statues guarding the temple. If they had seemed huge to Arthur from the balcony, then to Finn, standing outside the temple doors, they truly looked like stone gods.

"Come!" said Nefi, poking him in the ribs. "Let me show you inside!" Finn needed no second bidding. As an aspiring archaeologist, to see inside a vast, immaculate Theban temple would be an experience he would never forget.

And inside the temple was even more impressive than outside. An inner courtyard was surrounded by halls that were filled with vast stone pillars like huge tree trunks, which were carved with half-human, half-animal figures. The stone walls were brightly painted, the scenes illuminated by flaming torches. Somewhere unseen, a very deep, booming drum was being beaten. From time to time, between the columns, Finn would see shaven-headed, armed men, wearing white tunics emblazoned with the image of a golden sun.

"Here, follow me." Nefi took Finn by the hand and ran into one of the halls. They darted between the columns, dodging the occasional scowling temple guard, until they reached the perimeter wall. Nefi grabbed a flaming torch and led Finn along the wall, through a dark doorway and into a narrow passage. It now seemed to Finn that they were between two walls, or between two layers of the same wall.

"Come on," Nefi whispered as they jogged along. "This passage runs all around the temple. I can show you everything!" Finn could not remember ever being so excited by one of his and Arthur's missions. *Ancient Egypt! Secret temple passages and flaming torches and princesses and...*

His train of thought broke off as he bumped into Nefi. He was about to apologise when she turned to him, eyes very serious, and put a hand over his mouth. A few steps ahead Finn could see light on one of the walls, indicating another doorway, and through that doorway came snatches of a murmured conversation.

"... that it can never, never be traced back to the temple. That is the most important thing..."

"... will make sure the Nubians can take him easily, you have my word..."

"... maybe then finally he will see sense and allow us to make war on the Nubians. We have tolerated their presence for too long..."

Nefi's eyes grew even rounder, and she pushed Finn gently backwards until he understood what she wanted. He turned and began to creep back along the passage. They continued past the doorway through which they had entered and went on, around a corner, until Finn reckoned they must be inside the front wall of the temple. Sure enough they soon emerged beside the main entrance. Two temple guards cast sour glances at them as they made their way outside, but nobody tried to stop them.

"What was all that about?" Finn asked breathlessly once they were a safe distance from the temple.

"That was the high priest," said Nefi. "He has been trying to persuade the pharaoh to make war with the Nubians for months now. So far the pharaoh has resisted, partly because my mother is Nubian, but it sounds like the priest has devised some sort of plot. And that plot means war..."

CHAPTER 4

Ahead, the vultures were circling. The antelope carcasses had been carefully placed near a natural watering hole as bait for lions. A scattering of smaller animals was drinking at the hole, but so far there were no signs of larger prey.

"I still can't believe you hunt lions," said Arthur. He was standing beside Thami in a two-horse chariot.

"Why not?" Thami frowned. "How better to prove you are a man?"

Arthur looked over at Finn, who was standing with Nefi in the next chariot. Neither of them was comfortable with the idea of hunting animals for sport, and since Finn and Nefi had relayed what they'd heard in the temple, neither of them was comfortable with the idea of Thami being out in the middle of the desert. Whoever the priest had been speaking to had said he was going to 'make sure the Nubians can take him easily'. It didn't seem too much of a leap to imagine that 'he' was Thami, given what they knew from their briefing in the Hall of Heroes.

At first, when Thami had invited Finn and Arthur to come on a lion hunt, they had tried to dissuade him, but when they saw he was determined to go they had agreed to come as his guests. They were all too aware that, away from Thebes, accompanied only by a small group of the high priest's guards, Thami would be extremely vulnerable. It seemed highly likely that this was how he was destined to fall into Nubian hands, and if they could not stop him from going then they should go with him and try to limit the damage. Since overhearing the high priest's conversation in the temple, Nefi thought the same.

"There!" Thami hissed. The smaller animals at the watering hole were scattering with shrieks and grunts. A patch of sand seemed to detach itself from the floor, and a lioness darted towards the watering hole, making sure the other animals were well and truly driven away. She was followed by three other lionesses, and by one huge, dark-maned lion. He strolled boldly towards one of the antelope carcasses and lay down to eat while his pride kept watch and waited for their turn.

"So how do we kill them?" Arthur wondered out loud.

"First we try from here with arrows," said Thami. "Then if they escape, we give chase. They are fast, but cannot run for long. We chase them until they are exhausted, and then we strike."

Thami called over to Nefi, who relayed the message along a line of four more chariots, each of them manned by two temple guards. Slowly they began to advance. The lions looked up, alert to every strange sound, but they were not alarmed. They knew they were the kings of the desert.

Thami came to a halt and reached for one of the bows that were clamped to the side of his chariot, motioning Arthur to do the same. They were still at least fifty metres away, and hitting an animal from that distance seemed unlikely to Arthur, but along the line the hunters strung their bows, nocked their arrows and took aim. The first thing Arthur noticed was how powerful the bow felt, and it took all his strength to pull the string back to his shoulder. Aiming carefully wide of the lions, whom he had no wish to injure, Arthur waited for the instruction to shoot and then let his arrow fly safely to the side of one of the lionesses.

Despite a shower of arrows from the other hunters, not one lion was hit, but with angry snarls the lionesses darted away. The male, alone now, stood up from behind the antelope and faced the hunters, issuing an ear-splitting roar at the same time. Thami and the others were nocking their second arrows by this time, and the lion seemed suddenly alert to the danger, for he turned quickly and ran in the opposite direction.

Thami thrust his bow into Arthur's hands and urged his horses into action. The chariot lurched forward, almost throwing Arthur out of its open back. The other hunters did the same, and the hunt was on. Thami and Arthur led the chase, speeding across the desert as the lion sprinted towards a long line of rocky hills that seemed to sweep up out of the sand like an enormous wave-crest.

"If he reaches the hills our chariots will be useless!" Thami shouted.

From time to time the lion would stop to recover his breath and turn to look at his pursuers. The hunters shot a few arrows at him in those moments, though none found its mark. However each time the lion stopped the hunters were a little closer than the last time, and the arrows fell a little closer to their target. The lion was tiring and the hunters were closing in, but they were now so near to the hills that one more burst would take him onto the higher ground. The lion bounded on but was now clearly near exhaustion, and suddenly Thami and Arthur found themselves gaining on him rapidly.

Thami tied the reins together and slipped them over his back so that he wore them like a harness. "My bow!" he called, and Arthur

handed it over. Steering the horses now with his body, his hands free, Thami nocked an arrow and took aim. The lion stopped once more and turned, roaring with rage, making the horses suddenly veer wildly to the right. Thami's arrow flew harmlessly away as he dropped his bow and tried to regain control of the horses. But before he could do so, a wheel of the chariot hit a rock, the cart flew up in the air and the boys were hurled to the ground.

They landed some way apart, skidding to a painful stop in the dust. Both boys were badly winded and rolled around in pain. Blinking away tears, Arthur looked over to see that his friend was trying to stagger to his feet, clutching at a dagger he had withdrawn from his belt. Just a few metres away, the lion crouched, snarling, poised to spring at the prince.

Behind Thami, two chariots were racing to his aid. Nefi was in the lead, and she swerved with more control than Thami had done, while Finn stood poised to shoot an arrow at the lion. They swept past the scene of the crash and Finn let fly, his arrow fizzing over the lion's head. The beast roared again but did not flinch. Then came the second chariot. One of the guards held a spear poised and was shouting at the lion. But at the last moment, the lion finally turned and bounded towards safety at the boulder-strewn base of the hill.

The other chariots drew up, the guard lowered his spear, Thami slumped to the ground, and the danger was past.

* * *

"For as long as I can remember it has been Thami's desire to become a charioteer in my father's army. He takes any opportunity to hunt so he can practise his skills." Finn and Nefi were sitting by the campfire, going over the events of the day. The afternoon had passed uneventfully enough since the failed lion hunt, and the hunting party had set up camp in the open desert. The group had seemed subdued after Thami's near miss, and after an evening dinner around the campfire all but two temple guards, who were posted as sentries, and Finn and Nefi, who wanted to talk, had retired to their tents.

"'We will make sure the Nubians can take him easily,'" said Nefi quietly. "What if they mean Thami, Finn?" Finn said nothing. He wanted to reassure her but in truth he shared her fear. He and Arthur had discussed the same thing earlier that evening while the temple guards were making camp. They had agreed that Arthur would do his best to stay with Thami at all times so they had some chance of influencing events.

"If the Nubians were to capture Thami," Nefi went on, "it would force my father to do what so many of his advisers want – to make war against Nubia. I just know that the high priest is planning something awful."

Finn had to agree, although there was still much that didn't make sense. For one thing, he wondered, if the plan was to stage a kidnap, and assuming that the temple guards were part of the plot, why would they let Thami risk his life hunting lions? He would be no use to them dead.

"Another reason why that guard was so determined to drive the lion away!" said Nefi, keeping her voice low.

"I don't want to tempt fate," said Finn, "but if we're right about this plot then where better..."

He was interrupted by muffled shouts coming from the direction of the tent they were supposed to be sharing with Thami and Arthur. They scrambled to their feet and rushed back to it, both fearing the worst. Somewhere beyond the torches that ringed the camp they could hear horses' hooves disappearing into the distance.

Finn lifted back a flap of the tent and they both rushed inside. Nefi wailed. The tent was completely empty.

CHARIOTS

The Egyptians preferred using chariots to simple horse riding, especially when they went to war, and the pharaoh used the taxes he raised from the food that was grown in Egypt to pay for lots of chariot workshops.

The basic design of a chariot was a platform, quite low to the ground, which sat on two large wooden wheels, with a metal guard wall at about waist height running around the front and sides. This guard wall would have offered some protection against enemy spears and arrows as well as rocks kicked up by the wheels. It was also something to lean on or hang on to if things got really exciting!

The chariot was usually harnessed to two horses, who could then speed the charioteer around while charioteers were hunting or fighting. There were normally two people in each chariot. One would drive the horses, sometimes with his hands and sometimes with his body, by looping the reins around his waist. The other was a shield bearer, who would use his shield to protect both of them from enemy attack.

The most useful weapons for charioteers were bows and arrows and spears - weapons that could be used from a distance.

Chariots were expensive to make and expensive to maintain, not least because you needed two well-fed and well-trained horses. As a result, the charioteers were generally wealthy, elite soldiers, a little like European knights many centuries later.

CHAPTER 5

Arthur gasped when the blindfold was removed.

He had been in complete darkness from the moment that a sack had been pulled over his head. There had been no warning. No sounds of a scuffle. Somehow the kidnappers had floated past the temple guard sentries undetected. In fact the only voices Arthur could remember were those of Finn and Nefi calling out as they ran over from the campfire. When he and Thami cried out for help they were swiftly knocked unconscious, and by the time they came round they were each slung across the back of a horse, bound and blindfolded.

After several uncomfortable hours Arthur was dragged down off his horse and allowed to lie on a carpeted floor for a while, before being hauled to his feet again. He was marched up a long, steep flight of steps. He heard doors opening and closing, felt the ground beneath his feet become smoother, the air cooler and then warmer again, and then, with no warning at all, the blindfold was removed.

White-hot daylight stung his eyes and he cowered back from it, groaning. He was totally confused, having switched from night to day in an instant, and he began to panic, his breath coming in rapid, ragged gasps and his torso convulsing against the ropes that still bound his hands.

"Breathe deeply," he heard someone say and repeat over and over. Slowly he regained control and began to relax. He looked around and squinted through the bright light at Thami. "Breathe deeply," the boy kept saying. Arthur nodded. He began to take in a little more of his surroundings.

They were in a small courtyard, circled by smooth walls that looked to be covered in something like beige cement. The ground was bare earth, the same colour as the walls. In front of them was a huge man, his skin as dark as

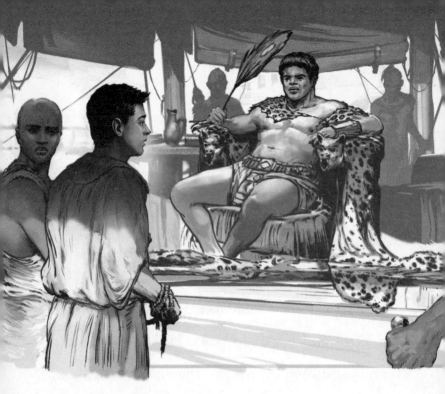

Thami's mother's. He was clearly very important. Most of the other men in the courtyard appeared to be soldiers who were standing rigidly to attention, while the big man was seated on a raised platform with an overhead screen shading him. He looked the boys up and down, one after the other, lazily swishing a fly swat around in one hand as he did so.

"You are Thamose," he said at length in a soft, low voice, waving the fly swat in Thami's direction, "son of the pharaoh of Egypt and his Nubian queen." He let the words hang in the air, and Arthur felt suddenly very conscious that he was at the heart of some very dangerous politics. "And do you, my prisoner, know who I am?"

Thami nodded and stared at the big man defiantly.

"You are the Nubian general, and this is your fortress in the western desert. What do you want with my friend and me?" Thami's royal breeding was showing. He sounded supremely confident, and the general chuckled.

"Why does a general take a prince captive?" the big man asked, smiling broadly.

"To start a war!" Arthur cut in, his senses now fully restored. Even as he said it, he knew it sounded stupid. Why would the Nubians actively seek to provoke Egypt, the most powerful kingdom in the region, maybe in the world, into open war?

Thami shook his head.

"You don't want a war, General, but that is what you'll get. You want to hold my father to ransom. You want him to agree payment of tributes to you in return for my release. Well, he won't do it!"

The general stood and looked down at Thami steadily. "You are a symbol, boy," he growled. "He won't pay tribute just for your life. He will pay tribute to prevent war. I know the pharaoh is weakened in his own palace by his closest advisers. They plot and scheme. The high priest wants one thing; the generals want another. Plenty of people want to overthrow your father. He can't risk going to war so he'll pay. My messengers are on their way to Thebes as we speak. You should pray that the pharaoh listens to them."

"You have been misled, General," said Thami. "Certainly there are those who wish to overthrow the pharaoh, and certainly the high priest is one of them, but that is not all he wants. He also wants Egypt to make war on Nubia. The high priest sees your presence here as an insult. You must know it is he who set up this kidnapping! He hopes to use it as a means of persuading my father to go to war, not to pay you tribute!"

"General, please," said a young man Arthur had not noticed before, stepping out from behind the platform. "This is what I was afraid of before the raid. Egypt is not as weak as our spies are being led to believe. We cannot risk a war – it could easily end in defeat for us and there are those in Thebes who long for that to happen. Even if we are not defeated we cannot conquer Egypt! We need not fall into the high priest's trap. Let the prisoners go now before it is too late. Think how many will die if we go to war..."

Doubt flickered across the general's face for a moment, but then he scowled.

"You question my judgement too much, Prince Shaharqo. I will always be loyal to your father but remember, military decisions are mine. Guards, take them!" He swished the fly swat at the boys as soldiers grabbed an arm each and led them away.

Arthur did his best to remember every detail of

the fortress as they were marched through it. The word 'fortress' had made him think of a castle, but as they were pushed along he soon realised they were in more of a fortified town than a castle. They walked along narrow, dusty lanes between terraced buildings, passing groups of soldiers at every turn, then up steps and eventually out onto the outer wall of the fortress, which was at least ten metres high. From here they could see out across the desert, although Arthur was surprised to observe that immediately around the fortress were trees and green fields.

"We are at one of the desert oases," said Thami, following Arthur's train of thought. "There is water here, hence the fortress."

They continued along the wall to a short, stubby tower, which they stooped to enter through a narrow doorway. From here the stairs led down again, and continued down by Arthur's reckoning to below ground level. At the bottom of the final flight of stairs the boys were pushed into a small, windowless room, lit by an oil lamp and furnished comfortably enough with rugs and cushions. Without a word, the guards cut the ropes that bound the boys' hands, then turned and re-climbed the stairs. They had passed no other doors onto the stairs as they went down, and Arthur concluded that the only way out was back up the tower and onto the fortress wall.

Deprived once again of natural light, the boys soon lost all sense of time. They were free to move around within the small cell and Arthur even ventured up the steps again but soon confirmed that, although they were not locked in, the only way out was the tiny doorway that linked the tower to the wall – and that had two armed guards outside it.

Arthur was alarmed to note that Thami's mood had deteriorated badly. Gone was the mask of regal confidence and authority he had displayed in front of the general, and the prince now lay sprawled in a corner, his face a picture of despair.

"This isn't over yet," said Arthur carefully, "and it's not your fault in any case."

Thami snorted. "I will be the reason that my mother's people and my father's people go to war. What else is there to say?" Already the horror that would haunt him for the next three thousand years was taking hold.

"Then we must try to escape," said Arthur briskly. "What we can't do is give up. You are a prince of Egypt, a son of the pharaoh, a hunter of lions and a future charioteer. We will fight this until it's over. Yes?"

Slowly Thami lifted his head and his gaze settled on Arthur. He seemed smaller than before, as if stooping beneath a great weight, but he gave Arthur the slightest of nods.

"Let's start by seeing if we can make a rope out of these rugs," said Arthur, keen to give them both something to do. The rugs were woven very tightly, and just to extract one row of thread was a painstaking task. To extract enough to twist into a long enough rope to descend from the fortress walls would take them days, and as they settled into working rhythms, the repetitive finger-picking had an almost soothing effect.

They worked in silence like this for a while,

and Arthur's thoughts turned for the first time to Finn. What would his brother be doing now? Had he been taken captive too? And what of Nefi? Better not let Thami start thinking like this, he thought, snapping back into his present environment.

"We should talk through exactly who is plotting what," he said abruptly. Thami looked up and nodded, and they began to discuss the possibilities. They kept coming back to the idea that the high priest was at the centre of the plot and that he had helped the Nubians kidnap Thami to provoke all-out war.

"But is the high priest hoping the war will damage the Nubians or your father?" Arthur wondered out loud.

"I think it's both," Thami replied. "He's always

made it obvious that he hates my mother and her people. And he would happily see the Nubians crushed. But most of all he wants to be rid of the pharaoh so that he can acquire more power for himself and the temple by helping someone else onto the throne. War suits him in every way."

"I wonder how the high priest managed to fool the general here so well. He seems clever enough..."

"I have been wondering exactly the same thing," said someone from the stairway. Both boys jumped and dropped the rugs they were working on. Whoever it was had come down the stairs without a sound. He stepped into the room and Arthur recognised him at once.

"Prince Shaharqo!" Thami exclaimed.

Arthur swallowed nervously. Had the prince

heard them talking about escape?

"It gives me no pleasure to see an Egyptian prince a prisoner here," said Shaharqo, and he seemed sincere. "I think that the general is being led into a trap, and unless someone stops him he is going to lead our whole army to war and a great many soldiers will die."

"Yes," said Thami desperately. "What did your spies suggest would happen if I were taken hostage?" Arthur grew hopeful. Maybe Shaharqo could be persuaded to let them go in secret.

"We were told that the high priest wanted to force the pharaoh into a position where he had to pay us tribute, and therefore would be seen as weak by others in Egypt. My father, the king of Nubia, thought it was an opportunity to enrich our kingdom."

"But the high priest hates Nubia," said Thami. "He has been pressing for war for months now. And I know my father. The Nile will run dry before he pays tribute to another king. We have to stop this. The only person who will benefit from a war is..."

"The high priest," they all said at once.

Arthur was overwhelmed by the size of the spider's web they were caught in. The idea that one person's political ambition and lies could be the reason for two kingdoms to go to war was almost too much to comprehend.

"There is something I should tell you, in the spirit of trust," said Shaharqo. "I led the raiding party to kidnap you. I did not like the plan, but I know my duty."

Thami shrugged. "That doesn't matter now," he said.

"I haven't finished. There were two other youths at the camp when we took you. A boy and a girl. I left a man behind to see what happened. He reports that the boy and the girl ran away from the camp. He tracked them because they weren't heading for Thebes. They were following us..."

CHAPTER 6

As they stood in the tent where their brothers had been sleeping, Finn and Nefi knew they had a matter of seconds to act.

"Come on," Nefi hissed. "If we stay we won't be able to do anything. If we run we may be able to help them." Finn needed no more convincing. Apart from everything else, he had no desire to stay with the temple guards now that Thami was no longer with them. They heard voices approaching outside, and Nefi rushed to the back of the tent and slashed at it with her knife. Finn followed her through the cut and out into the night. Stooping low, they ran towards the tethered horses. One of the men was keeping watch over the animals, guarding against hyenas or anything else that might attack in the night. Nefi and Finn dropped to the ground behind a small ridge of earth but as they did so the shouts of the men near the tent caught the guard's attention and he ran towards his friends. The horses, sensing something was up, were grinding their teeth and pawing at the ground.

Nefi chose the two that were calmest and cut their tethering ropes before leaping up onto one of them. They were much smaller than modern horses, but nonetheless Finn struggled to get on as there was no saddle and no stirrups. After two failed attempts Nefi brought her horse alongside and reached out a hand to help Finn onto his.

"They're gone!" one of the guards shouted from the other side of the camp. "The boy and the girl are gone!"

Finn and Nefi kicked their horses into action and sped away.

From time to time it seemed to Finn that they were being followed.

They had left the camp far behind, and Nefi had found her way back to the line of hills that the lion had escaped into the previous day. Once they had gained the upper ridge line,

Nefi said all they had to do was follow it until morning and they would arrive at the oasis.

The moon had disappeared, but although the desert sky seemed to be filled with more stars than Finn had ever imagined, they did not provide enough light to see by. Certainly there was no hunting party coming after them, but now and again Finn was sure he could hear another horse's hooves. Each time, they would rein their horses in and listen and each time there would be no sound, but the feeling would not go away until finally they heard, below them rather than behind, the sound of a solitary rider overtaking them and speeding ahead towards the Nubian fortress.

Finn and Nefi stared at one another, dismayed. It seemed too much of a coincidence to hope that the unknown rider was doing anything other than reporting their approach to the Nubians. They dismounted, both suddenly exhausted. They had not slept all night and the adrenaline that had kept them going so far left them empty now they knew they were not being followed by the temple guards. They had no food or water, and no shelter, but pressing ahead towards an enemy who knew they were coming seemed foolish. They sat huddled together with the blankets from the horses' backs around their shoulders. Finn was amazed by how cold he now felt, when during the day the desert was almost too hot to bear.

"We were stupid to think we could help," he said glumly. "We should have let the guards take us back to Thebes."

"They would never have let us warn my father though. They'd have killed us before letting that happen. We had to run. All we can do for now is try to survive. Anyway, get some sleep. We'll need energy tomorrow if we're going to make it." Nefi lay down and Finn did the same, and they both drifted into a restless, uncomfortable half-sleep.

Finn woke, throat parched and sore, as the sky began to lighten with the first approaches of dawn. He looked over at Nefi, who was snoring softly, and rubbed his eyes in astonishment. Beyond where she lay, the ground fell gently away, sloping down towards the desert floor. Except it wasn't the desert he could see. Unknowingly, they had stopped at the end of the range of hills and ahead, in plain sight,

lay a lake. It was surrounded by a belt of vegetation that was dotted with small clusters of mud-brick houses and beyond its opposite bank, rising up out of the desert, was a fortified town.

Gently, he shook Nefi awake and pointed. As soon as she saw the oasis she leapt to her feet.

"We should get down there for water now. The later we leave it the more people will see us."

They folded their blankets up and draped them over the horses' backs, then clambered up and began to pick their way down towards the oasis. They were about half way down when the slope steepened and the horses became extremely anxious. Nefi slipped to the ground and Finn was about to follow suit when he caught sight of a young lion, watching from a rock to the side of them. Worse, the horses saw the lion at the same moment. Both of them whinnied and reared, and Finn was thrown onto the rocks as they bolted. He landed awkwardly and let out a yelp of pain as his foot cracked against hard stone.

The lion, tail swishing, stayed on its perch.

Nefi rushed to Finn's side and helped him up. Finn looked around at the lion in panic.

"Don't worry about him," she soothed. "They don't usually attack, as long as you keep out of their way. Can you walk?"

Finn took a single tentative step and yelped again.

"Come," said Nefi, putting Finn's arm over her shoulder. "We'll walk together."

The lion watched with lazy interest as they hobbled away, and although he did not follow them, Finn once again found himself looking nervously over his shoulder at regular intervals.

"What are we going to do?" he croaked, all moisture in his mouth now long gone.

"The first thing is to get water," said Nefi. "Then we can think further ahead." Neither of them voiced their concerns, though they had plenty. Their greatest problem was that one of them couldn't walk and the horses had run away. How would they get back to Thebes?

By the time they reached the edge of the lake, the sun was beginning to float up from the horizon, warming the air almost immediately. They drank deeply and washed the dirt from their faces, and slowly they began to feel a little more alive. Finn washed his bad foot, squeezing it and poking at it gingerly. At no point on the way down had he felt like he was going to be able to walk off the injury and he knew that it was likely he had fractured a bone.

"So, what are we going to do?" Finn asked again. But before Nefi could answer they heard a young voice behind them.

"Have you travelled from far?" The voice belonged to a boy of eight or nine years. He had a curved stick, a bit like a boomerang, in one hand and a pair of dead birds in the other. "I was hunting with my throwing stick and I saw you walk down. Did you sleep in the hills?" Nefi nodded.

"Then you should come with me. My mother will give you food. You want food?" Nefi and Finn looked at one another. They had little choice but to trust the boy. They needed food, and here was someone offering it.

"Where do you live, little one?" Nefi asked.

"Hey! I'm not so little. I killed the food you'll eat, remember that!" he replied. "I'm Caro by the way, and I live in the village on this side of the lake."

Caro kept up a steady chatter as he led the hobbling pair towards one of the groups of mud huts that Finn had noticed earlier, and presently to a door and into one of the houses.

"Mother! Travellers!" Caro shouted as Finn and Nefi glanced around. They were in a modest but clean room with rush matting on the floor. Off to one side there appeared to be a kitchen, and to the rear some sort of garden area. It came as a surprise to Finn when he noticed stairs up to another floor. Caro's mother came down and looked at her new guests warily.

"They came from the hills, Mother. The boy has hurt his foot and they don't have any food."

"What happened?" she asked.

"We were travelling with friends near Thebes," said Finn quickly, going on to explain that their camp had been attacked and he and Nefi had escaped on horseback. He didn't mention the kidnapping.

"So you are Egyptian then?" the woman asked. There seemed little point trying to offer a different story, and they both nodded.

"Caro," she said to her son, "go and find your father out in the fields and tell him that I need to speak to him but do it quietly. Don't tell anyone about our guests just yet."

Finn could have hugged her, and she saw the

relief in his and Nefi's faces.

"Well, whoever you are you have suffered and you must rest here and let me feed you."

She began busying herself with food preparations and the two travellers settled down on floor cushions. Finn realised that rescuing Arthur and Thami was almost impossible now, but they had made it to the oasis, they were in sight of the fortress and so all was not lost. When Caro's mother placed a bowl of something rather similar to porridge in front of him, he began to feel that things were looking up.

They were half way through their meal when Caro returned with his father, who seemed remarkably relaxed about having two strangers as guests in his house. He listened carefully as Caro and his wife explained what they knew of the travellers and said nothing for a while when they had finished.

"There is a rumour," he said at length, "that two Egyptian prisoners were taken in the desert last night and brought to the fortress."

EXTRACT FROM *WARRIOR HEROES*
BY FINN BLADE

WHO DID WHAT?

Of course most people in ancient Egypt were not princes and did not live in palace complexes! Here is a list of social groups, starting with the smallest and most elite, and ending with the one that included the largest number of people.

1. Pharaoh - He was believed by many to be a living god, in touch with the other gods who controlled the universe and who decided when the Nile would flood, and therefore when to bring famine and when to bring prosperity.

2. Nobles and priests - The priests

helped the pharaoh to honour the gods properly to help protect the people. The pharaoh's government was made up entirely of nobles. Really the priests and nobles were like extensions of the pharaoh's authority.

3. Soldiers - Commanded by the pharaoh, soldiers were the next extension of his power, fighting off outside threats, stopping internal uprisings and, during times of peace, supervising the great building projects of Egypt.

4. Scribes - Running an empire required the Egyptians to develop into skilled accountants and organisers. The scribes were the people who kept all the records

and wrote everything down to make
sure that affairs were kept in
order.

5. Artisans and merchants - They
made and traded things other than
crops.

5. Farmers and slaves - They did
the hard work of growing all the
food that Egypt relied on for life
and wealth.

CHAPTER 7

By the middle of the third day, Arthur and Thami had a rope that was easily twenty metres long. They had taken turns at the top of the stairs through each night, watching and waiting for the guards to fall asleep and give them a chance to escape, but the men seemed too well drilled for that.

"If Shaharqo is a prince then why doesn't he

do something?" Thami grumbled, kicking out at the half-destroyed carpet.

"You have to admit it's very risky for him," said Finn. Shaharqo had been convinced that they were all victims of the high priest's schemes and he said he would help if he could. But it was clear that the general's mind was made up and he believed Egypt had no stomach for war. Unless the boys could escape, the Nubians would try to blackmail the pharaoh and the result would be a bloody war that would condemn Thami to a never-ending, restless, guilt-ridden afterlife.

This dark circle of thoughts was broken by the sound of footsteps above them. Thami and Arthur leapt to their feet. Other than a silent guard who crept down the stairs twice a day to give them food and drink they had seen nobody since Shaharqo's visit. Arthur prayed that it would be the prince returning with a plan, and for a moment he thought his prayers were answered as Shaharqo appeared at the bottom of the stairs.

Thami began to speak but Shaharqo held up his hand to silence him. The prince's expression was cold and hard, and behind him followed four guards.

"The general wishes to speak with you once more," said Shaharqo as the guards took up their places behind the boys, one man holding each arm. Arthur's mind spun as they retraced their steps along the fortress wall and through the town to the same small courtyard where they had first encountered their captor. What had changed? Did the general want to question them more about the high priest? Could they talk him round, or could this be their opportunity to escape?

As before the general sat on a raised platform. In fact the only difference to the scene was the addition of a large and very intimidating battle mace. Arthur couldn't take his eyes off the huge, spiked club. Suddenly his throat felt very dry.

"The news is not good," the general began. "The pharaoh has refused our terms, and he has sent word that should I fail to release you, he will interpret my actions as a declaration of war."

Arthur looked over at Thami, but the prince remained silent and his face revealed nothing.

"It is possible that what you have told me about the high priest is correct," the general went on. Arthur could hardly believe his ears.

"All I heard when you spoke earlier was a prisoner bargaining for his release. But I admit I should have considered your advice more carefully, Prince Shaharqo."

"Well you have it in your power to put a stop to all this..." Shaharqo began, though he trailed off as the general shook his head wearily.

"There is too much honour at stake now. We took the boys hostage; we sent the demands for the pharaoh to pay tribute. If we back down now we will be weakened for generations. The armies on both sides are being mustered. It has to be so."

Thami and Shaharqo began to protest, but the general would not listen.

"I brought you here simply to tell you that you will be held hostage for the duration of the war. Guards, take them back."

The boys were marched in stunned silence back to their cell. Shaharqo stayed behind after the guards had climbed back up out of the tower.

"Don't give up hope," said Shaharqo. "This can still be stopped. We just have to find a way of exposing the high priest as the snake that he is."

"That man is using me as a way of starting a war," Thami growled. "Snake? I'll feed him to the snakes!" Arthur and Shaharqo let him carry on in this way until his rage subsided.

"But if I can find a way to get you back to Thebes," Shaharqo said eventually. "Would you be able to denounce the high priest?"

When Shaharqo returned that night, the boys were surprised to see him dressed not as a prince or a soldier but as a rather shabby commoner.

"We could persuade the pharaoh if the high priest were to admit his own guilt," said Shaharqo before either of them could comment. "But that will not happen."

Thami and Arthur had spent hours discussing how they would go about proving that the high priest had lied to everyone. They knew that simply telling the pharaoh was not enough. At the moment there was no proof. If Thami suddenly reappeared in Thebes and denounced the high priest, the priest would simply say that the Nubians had made up a ridiculous story as a way of pulling back from the conflict. Result? War as planned. Nefi had overheard someone she thought was the high priest talking about 'taking him'? Too vague.

"However there is one other way," said Shaharqo.

"If the pharaoh heard the full story of the high priest's deceit from the Nubian point of view, if we can identify our own spies and show how the high priest tricked them to provoke war, it is just possible that we will prevent it." The Nubian prince placed the three bags on the floor, opened them, and began sifting through the contents: food, water skins, cloaks and blankets.

"Are you going to let us escape?" Thami asked, not quite daring to believe his eyes.

"He's not just going to let us escape," said Arthur, looking at the three bags. "He's coming with us!"

"And I have another surprise for you," said Shaharqo, beaming at them. "But you'll have to wait until we get beyond the wall for that." The sudden change in their circumstances was a lot to take in and the boys sat and listened, slightly in awe, as their captor-turned-saviour described his plans. There was a cart and horses waiting a short distance away from the fortress and, all being well, by the time anyone noticed their absence they would already be in Thebes.

"Does anyone know what you are doing?" Arthur asked.

Shaharqo shook his head. "I have soldiers loyal to me who have helped me with arrangements but they asked no questions. There are no guards upstairs for this watch, and although they might suspect that this is in order to let you escape, they do not know that I am going with you."

Thami began to suggest more details of their strategy once they got to Thebes, but Shaharqo cut him off.

"We will discuss these things once we are safely away from this fortress, yes?"

Thami nodded, and extended his arms to embrace Shaharqo and Arthur at once.

"Whatever happens, we are all brothers now," said the Egyptian. "And we have a war to stop!"

They put on their cloaks, grabbed a bag each and Shaharqo led them up the stairs and out into the night. The air was cool and clear, the stars bright, and the boys were fizzing with nervous energy. They followed Shaharqo along the fortress wall and down onto the street below where he pointed at three buckets placed at the bottom of the wall.

"One each," said Shaharqo. "They have nets in them. We are fishermen heading down to the lake."

Hooded now and covering their faces as they scurried through a labyrinth of lanes and alleyways, the boys carried their bags and buckets after Shaharqo, and soon they saw they were approaching a fortified gatehouse. For a moment the boys' hearts sank as they saw that the huge gates were bolted shut, but as they approached a guard looked them up and down and then, without saying a word, opened a small door that formed part of one of the gates. They stepped through, the door closed behind them, and they were free.

It was all Arthur could do not to laugh out loud with relief, but he kept his cool and set off after Shaharqo along the road that led down towards the lake. At first the road was empty but after a while they saw a band of around twenty Nubian soldiers coming towards them. The man at the front of the band turned his head as they drew level and seemed about to speak, but then decided better of it and the danger passed.

They smelled the wet mud and the reeds before they saw the lake in the dark, and then they followed the road that ran directly alongside the lake for a while. Shaharqo stopped beside a small thicket of trees and emitted a low whistle. From somewhere behind the trees they heard horses, harnesses and wheels and a moment later a man emerged, leading two horses and a large cart.

"The night is young," said the man.

"And the oasis is old," Shaharqo replied, keeping his face well covered. The man nodded, happy with this response, and handed the reins over to the prince before disappearing back into the night. Shaharqo climbed onto the cart, the two boys stepped up behind him, the horses turned their noses east, and the journey back to Thebes began.

CHAPTER 8

They veered away from the lake, staying close to the line of hills that Finn and Nefi had ridden along the top of. Shaharqo explained that the hills would guide them most of the way to Thebes, and that a steady trot through the night should be enough to get them across the desert before dawn. Arthur suggested that they take shifts driving the horses while the others slept but Shaharqo told them to stay awake for now. This seemed odd to Arthur, but the reason soon became clear. Barely five minutes after leaving the lake, Shaharqo brought the cart to a stop and sent out another low whistle.

A young boy emerged from behind a boulder, beckoning to somebody behind him. Two cloaked, shadowy figures followed the boy towards the cart, one hobbling badly and leaning on a shepherd's crook. Arthur and Thami trusted Shaharqo but still they tensed as the strangers approached.

"Thami!" one of them called out softly in a familiar voice. "Help your sister up, you lazy old donkey!" The two hobbling figures stopped behind the cart and pulled their hoods back. To Arthur and Thami's utter delight, they found themselves staring down at Nefi and Finn.

"I told you I had a surprise for you!" said Shaharqo as the siblings hugged one another. "But hurry! We must get to Thebes undetected, and we must stop this war before it has started."

"Yes, we must go!" said Thami.

"Goodbye, Caro!" Nefi called as the cart began rolling. "Thank you." But the boy had already disappeared and everyone settled down in the back of the cart. Thami told his sister and Finn about all that had happened since their capture, and about their plan to expose the high priest.

"But what about you?" Arthur asked when Thami had finished. "How did you end up here?"

Finn told the story of their overnight journey along the hilltops, pausing, embarrassed, at the part where the horses bolted.

"So I carried him down to the water's edge," said Nefi, picking up the story much to Arthur's amusement. She soon had the whole cart laughing with her exaggerated impressions of Finn's yelps and moans.

"But how did you find us?" Arthur asked eventually. Nefi replied that Caro's father had assumed they were all part of the same hunting party as he had heard from soldier friends of two hostages being brought in from the desert the night before they arrived. Shaharqo had asked the soldier who had tracked Nefi and Finn to put out word on the quiet that he was looking for a boy and a girl from the hills, and they had soon been tracked down. Then when the escape was set, Shaharqo had sent a message to Caro's father that his guests were in danger and would be taken away to safety if they met him by the side of the road at the appointed time.

Conversation soon turned to the group's plans for Thebes. It was agreed that they would all need to enter the palace in secret. In order to benefit from the element of surprise it was crucial that the high priest should not know they had returned until the moment of confrontation. This would be challenging as the temple guards, who operated throughout the palace and temple complex, would be sure to report back to the high priest as soon as either Thami or Nefi was recognised.

After much deliberation, it was decided that they would lay their trap in the Valley of the Kings, where the pharaoh's tomb was being hewn into the rocks. Work had been going on for several years, but the pharaoh took every opportunity to check on its progress, and Thami felt sure that if war was imminent then a visit to the tomb would be on the pharaoh's mind.

They agreed that Finn, Thami and Shaharqo would hide in the valley while Arthur and Nefi continued to the palace to try and reach the queen. They would tell the queen everything, and enlist her help in persuading the pharaoh to bring the high priest to the tomb, where they would confront him.

Plans thus outlined, they settled down beneath blankets in the back of the cart, with Shaharqo promising to wake Thami and change places with him midway through the journey.

Arthur, for one, did not feel tired. He was all too aware that the whole plan relied on him and

Nefi getting into the palace undetected by the temple guards. Also, he was troubled by the very idea of the high priest, a man he had never met, yet one who was pulling the strings of two kingdoms and steering them towards a war that could cost thousands of lives. The prospect of meeting such a man, let alone confronting and defeating him, was daunting indeed and when he finally drifted away his sleep was darkly restless.

Arthur jolted awake to the sound of raised Egyptian voices.

"And where have you come from?" someone demanded.

"We were separated from my master, an oil merchant, travelling along the oasis route," Shaharqo replied. Arthur pulled the blanket down off his face and noticed that the sky was beginning to pale. "We hope to rejoin my master at Thebes."

"You are a Nubian!" said somebody else. "And your general holds captive one of the pharaoh's sons and has killed one of his daughters. Why should we not kill you now, just as we will kill your brothers on the battlefield?"

So they think Nefi was killed in the raid... thought Arthur.

"Sirs, please!" Shaharqo whined. "I am my master's slave. You have many Nubians in Thebes, no? What the general does has nothing to do with the rest of us."

"He's right!" said Thami, sitting up in the back of the cart. "This man belongs to my father, who we are hoping to meet in Thebes. You are

soldiers. You must see that we are not soldiers!"

"And what about this pale creature?" said one of the men, gesturing in Arthur's direction as he too sat up.

"My father adopted him on his travels," Thami lied smoothly. There were four soldiers standing at the front of the cart, but looking around Arthur could see they were in big trouble. Their route had taken them into a valley, bounded on one side by the line of hills they had been following from the oasis, and on the other by a second, converging ridge. The men questioning them were Egyptian sentries, behind whom were row upon row of tents. Looking up to the ridge lines on either side of them, Arthur could see more tents along the tops of the hills. Shaharqo had driven the cart straight into the middle of an Egyptian army camp!

The soldiers whispered to one another. Finn and Nefi were awake too by this time, and all five of the travellers were now sitting up in the cart, waiting nervously to learn their fate. Finally one of the sentries ordered them down from the cart.

"You will wait until after sunrise when we will speak to our captain."

Thami began to protest but was cut short.

"Do as you are commanded, or it will be worse for you!" There was little choice but to obey, so they climbed down from the cart and allowed two of the sentries to steer them into a large, empty tent. The guards remained outside, and the five travellers were forced to accept the possibility that their adventure might be over.

"I am sorry," said Shaharqo, slumping down on the floor. Thami was unforgiving.

"How did you not see the danger?" he hissed. "And why didn't you wake me in the night as we agreed?"

"I did not realise it was so late," Shaharqo replied gloomily. "Suddenly it was almost dawn and the camp was right there in front of us..."

"It would have happened whoever had been driving," said Nefi. "We picked the straightest route from the oasis to Thebes. We should have known our father might already have posted his advance guard here."

Thami relented, although Shaharqo remained disconsolate. Soon the sounds of the rest of the camp beginning to wake up drifted in through the walls of the tent.

"We should be quiet in case anyone overhears us," said Finn. "And we should listen to the soldiers' conversations. We may learn something useful about what is going on in Thebes."

"Yes," Thami agreed, nodding enthusiastically. "That is a very good suggestion." Finn soaked up the praise. It was the first time he had felt useful since falling off his horse.

They lay down as if resting, and listened attentively to the chatter of the wakening camp. In amongst the coarse joking and practical communication they gleaned three valuable pieces of information. First, an army of nearly five thousand men had already been mustered from Thebes and the surrounding farmland. Second, the pharaoh himself had decided to lead his army into battle. And third, later that day the high priest would conduct sacred rites in the palace temple in Thebes before blessing the pharaoh and his army. In hushed whispers, the group changed their plans to focus instead on the blessing ceremony.

Without warning, a lean, grizzled man

entered the tent followed by the sentry who had detained them. He cast an irritated eye over the group on the floor of the tent.

"Idiot!" he barked at the sentry. "Is this what a Nubian attack looks like? Let them go at once."

THE GODS

The Egyptians worshipped a huge number of gods - nobody really knows how many. Here is a list of some of the best-known ones.

1. Amen-Ra - Appearing as a man with a hawk's head, Amen-Ra was really a combination of two gods - Ra, the great sun god, and Amen, the local god of Thebes. The Egyptians believed that he was reborn every day with the sunrise, sailed across the sky during the day, and every night did battle with the forces of chaos in the underworld!

2. Sobek - The crocodile god of the Nile, Sobek had the body of a

man and the head of a crocodile. He controlled the waters of the Nile and he represented the might of the pharaoh; he was fiercely protective of his children and lethal to his enemies.

3. Osiris - Believed to be the first pharaoh of Egypt, Osiris married his sister, Isis. He was killed by his brother, Set, who chopped him up into lots of bits and distributed the body parts along the Nile.

4. Isis - Legend told that after her brother and husband Osiris had been killed by Set, Isis travelled the length of Egypt to find the parts of his body and bound them back together with cloth, creating

the first mummy. Osiris became the god of the dead!

5. Set – The murderous brother of Osiris and Isis. Their son Horus defeated Set, though, who was banished and became the god of the desert.

CHAPTER 9

As they trundled out of the camp, the group put the finishing touches to their plan. Arthur and Nefi would aim to reach the queen as previously agreed. The other three would try to find the Nubian spies, whose evidence would help persuade the pharaoh that the high priest was manipulating everyone. They would then converge on the blessing ceremony at the temple, when the high priest could be denounced in public. They would follow Thami's lead when it came to the moment of confrontation.

Shaharqo continued to drive as he was the least likely to be recognised by any temple guards who had strayed beyond the palace complex. They reached the brow of a small hill and from there they could see their route descending steadily towards the western side of Thebes, and behind it the Nile. Shaharqo brought the cart to a halt and they stared at the scene. On the river they could see dozens of huge barges, crowded with men, and from the banks of the river at various points there snaked long lines of soldiers, some on foot, some in chariots, all heading towards them. There were thousands on the march already.

"This is what your general is going to lead his men against," said Thami.

"No," said Shaharqo hoarsely. "We will stop it."

They pressed forward towards Thebes, and soon were carving through a tide of Egyptian soldiers coming the other way. Arthur was surprised at how many of them were Nubian, judging by their dark skin, but Shaharqo said that even if they were of Nubian origin, those who lived in Egypt thought of themselves as Egyptian.

At length they reached the first of the temples of Thebes, and here they were able to get away from the swarming army. Shaharqo brought the cart to a halt and they all climbed down. They agreed to split into their two groups immediately so that if one were caught the other might still have a chance to reach the pharaoh. Shaharqo reached into the cart and ripped away a panel from the inside to reveal a stash of weapons. He handed swords to the boys, and passed a dagger to Nefi, and they each took a final drink from a water skin. Then, after wishing each other good luck, they set off in different directions.

Finn made good speed leaning on his shepherd's crook, but it was hard work and he was soon sweating and panting as he tried to keep pace with the others. Thami was asking about the spies.

"We have two loyal Nubian men who are servants to the temple guard," Shaharqo confirmed.

"Then we will start by going to the temple

barracks," said Thami. "That is where they are most likely to be. When we get there Finn and I will stay hidden – the guards may recognise us despite the dust and my ordinary clothes. You will need to ask after the spies, Shaharqo."

Finn wanted to know what they would do if they couldn't find the spies at the barracks.

"We won't keep looking for them," said Thami. "They will make it easier to persuade my father but they are not essential. If we don't find them we will head straight for the palace temple of Amen, stay hidden and wait for the ceremony." It all sounded very easy.

Five minutes later they arrived at a long, simple, flat building.

"This is it," said Thami. "You ask at that door. We'll wait around the back."

Shaharqo stepped forward and knocked. There were footsteps from within and the other two turned and began walking away, following one side of the building. They heard Shaharqo ask for the spies by name, and he was told to wait at the door.

Finn glanced back over his shoulder before they turned the corner. He saw Shaharqo being ushered inside just as he and Thami disappeared behind the barracks. They were well hidden and in shade, with a windowless wall on one side and a high bank of earth on the other creating a narrow corridor barely two metres wide.

There they crouched down and waited. To begin with they didn't speak but concentrated instead on any sound of disturbance coming from the barracks. But as the minutes passed, their uncertainties grew. Was Shaharqo in trouble? Should they have tried to find the spies in the first place? Worst of all, what would they do if Shaharqo didn't come back?

Their questions were answered when they heard the door open. Finn peered around the corner, careful to keep his body well hidden by the building, and stiffened. Striding towards them were two temple guards.

He darted back out of sight and motioned to Thami to run the other way along the back wall. They fled as fast as Finn's foot would allow, drawing their swords as they did so. They were half way along the length of the wall when they heard shouts behind them. Finn risked a glance back and saw that there were now four guards following them, swords drawn, running hard. Then there were more shouts, this time from in front.

With a sick feeling in his stomach, Finn turned to see yet more guards coming towards them from up ahead. With the barracks wall on one side and the natural bank on the other they were completely trapped. Putting up a fight was obviously useless, and the boys wisely threw down their weapons as the guards approached. There was no recognition on any of their faces. Perhaps they were so used to seeing Thami in princely attire that this battered, dirty, travel-weary youth seemed a different type of person entirely. In any case, there were no words. The first guards grabbed each boy by the shoulders, and the next thing Finn knew was the nasty sensation of a hood being pulled over his eyes, followed by a sharp blow to the head, and complete darkness.

* * *

While this was happening, Arthur and Nefi were following the banks of the Nile towards the point where they had landed the night they first met. There seemed little chance of them being recognised. For one thing Arthur was now covered in so much dirt that his skin was no longer pale, and Nefi's once-white linen dress was so grimy it was impossible to imagine that she was a princess. Her green eye paint had long since been washed away, and the pair of them looked just like the hundreds of other busy figures who jostled their way along the banks of the river.

"Why are there so many people here?" Nefi wondered out loud. "This side of the river is usually for people on royal business only."

"War. We're all on royal business now,"

replied a passer-by, barely turning his head.

As they neared the palace complex they grew ever more alert to the danger of being spotted. But when a group of temple guards strolled past they did not give the grubby pair a second glance. Listening to other people's conversations on the way they learned that the high priest was to bless the pharaoh and the war within the hour. The crowds of people that Arthur and Nefi were part of had been shipped across from Eastern Thebes to witness the blessing, and they were all heading for the palace complex.

They followed the surging crowd into the square at the heart of the royal buildings, and straight ahead of them they saw the palace temple, its painted stone guards towering over the crowd. They were about to head for the door into the queen's quarters when Arthur's eye was caught by a flash of dazzling green.

"Wait! Look!" he cried, pointing to the temple entrance. There, sitting on a podium near the base of one of the statues alongside two other women, was the Nubian queen.

"Mother..." Nefi whispered.

Arthur's mind raced. "If we go to her now the high priest will know what's coming. We have to wait until the ceremony starts, and then find a way through."

Nefi thought for a moment. "I know a way. Follow me."

She led Arthur towards the palace, which bordered one side of the square. A small alleyway cut through the building and on the other side, where it was far less crowded, Arthur found that they were now looking at the back of the building. Nefi headed towards an unassuming little doorway. A temple guard was positioned on each side of the door, looking on as a cart full of loaves of bread was unloaded and servants began to carry the bread inside, balancing baskets on their heads. They were overseen not just by the guards, but also by a tall Nubian woman, who seemed to be in charge. Nefi was visibly delighted.

"That's my mother's cook," she said quietly. "She'll help us!" And before Arthur could stop her, Nefi had run across to the cook and grabbed her arm. Arthur stayed back, unsure what to do, but whatever conversation passed between Nefi and the cook seemed to work. Nefi beckoned Arthur over to join them and, her face betraying not the slightest surprise, the cook casually handed a basket each to Nefi and Arthur, and herded them inside.

"It is good to see you alive, little one," said the cook once they had found a quiet space. "Everyone but your mother believed you were dead!"

"It is good to see you too, Mery," Nefi replied. "But we have no time to speak. The pharaoh is in danger. The whole kingdom is in danger and we can help. Just don't tell anyone that you have seen us. Promise!"

"Of course, little one. But wait, before you go there are things you should know. Your mother fears for her life now that Nubia and Egypt are at war. She tells me that the high priest has tried to persuade the pharaoh that she is loyal to Nubia. If you are trying to reach her in secret it will not be easy. She is watched constantly by the temple guards." The woman's face was creased with worry, and she held both of Nefi's hands tightly in her own.

"I have a way," was all Nefi said. "Come with me, Arthur."

They ran along a sequence of servants' corridors at the bottom and to the rear of the palace, passing only the occasional servant on the way, until Nefi turned sharply and led the way upstairs and out into a grand chamber. Arthur's jaw dropped at the riches on display. Everything seemed to be made of gold. Even the bed at one end of the room was painted in gold leaf.

"The pharaoh's chambers," Nefi said. "Unguarded while the pharaoh is in the temple for the blessing. Hurry." She lifted a torch off its wall hanging and stepped up onto the golden bed, reaching a hand up and pressing the nose of a jackal that was carved into the wall above. A panel slid open to reveal the opening to a hidden passage. They stepped through and Nefi pushed the door closed behind her.

"There are lots of secret passages in the palace," she explained and then dashed ahead before Arthur could ask where they were going. They followed the passage down some stairs and then on in a long straight line for perhaps fifty metres before they came to a fork.

"That way to escape the palace," said Nefi breathlessly. "This way to the temple."

On they ran, through the dark passage, until more stairs led them up to a different type of passage. Stone walls towered above them on both sides.

"We're inside the outer wall of the temple," Nefi said softly. "We'll have to keep quiet now." She slowed down and they crept forward. They could see light at the end of the passage.

"That's the entrance to the temple," Nefi whispered. They saw robed figures passing across the opening to the passage, though they were far enough away still that it was impossible to make out any details. Then they heard the roar of the crowd. They stole forward, on and on until they were positioned just inside the passage, crouching down and peering out of the entrance.

To one side Arthur could see the temple courtyard, surrounded by the halls of columns. To the other side he saw, from behind, ranks of temple guards and in front of them a huge shaven-headed man in white robes emblazoned with the same sun symbol as worn by the palace guards. His arms were spread wide as he encouraged the crowd to ever-louder cheers.

"And the gods have spoken to me of VICTORY! VICTORY! VICTORY!"

"The high priest," Nefi spat. Through the legs of the guards, Arthur could see that the queens on their raised platform were on the priest's right, and to his left stood a huge throne.

Must be where the pharaoh is, thought Arthur.

"What now?" he whispered.

"We go to my mother. The priest's attention will be on my father. Come!"

They emerged from the passage and crept behind the guards and around the base of one of the statues.

"And the gods have decreed that your pharaoh will lead the army himself!" cried the priest triumphantly. The crowd roared its approval once more.

"Mother!" Nefi hissed as soon as she was near enough. The queen turned her head and her eyes widened. Nefi and Arthur made a break for it. They sprinted across the last few metres to the queen's side.

The cheering in the crowd was replaced by gasps.

"Assassins!" cried one of the temple guards as a group of them lurched towards Arthur and Nefi. The crowd had gone completely silent.

"NO!" shouted the queen. "It is Princess Nefru, the pharaoh's daughter. You will NOT harm these children!"

The high priest turned to them with a face like a desert lightning storm.

"SEIZE THEM!" he roared.

CHAPTER 10

The pharaoh slowly stood, his chest shimmering with gold, and his bulbous blue and gold hat giving him the appearance of a giant. In one hand he held a whip. In the other, a shepherd's crook.

"Come to me!" he said, his arms outstretched. "I was told you were dead, my child."

Nefi ran towards him but the high priest

stepped in front and grabbed her.

"Let her go!" Arthur shouted, though before he had taken a step he was held fast by two temple guards, as was the queen beside him. "The high priest arranged for Thami to be kidnapped by the Nubians. He told them where to find him and he told them that you would pay tribute for his return rather than risk war. All the high priest wants is war. War and to see you overthrown!"

"Silence, snake!" the high priest snarled. "Have I not warned you, Majesty, that your Nubian queen and her children cannot be trusted any more than her people in the desert? Can you not see what is happening? Nefru was kidnapped with her brother rather than killed as we first thought. Now when the Nubians realise that they have made a big mistake in doubting your power, your wrath, Majesty, they send the girl back with this story to try and save their worthless skins."

The queen implored both men to let Nefru go, but the pharaoh seemed paralysed by doubt, and the high priest began to press his case.

"Did we not discover two Nubian spies, Majesty, serving in our own temple? And when we had tortured them, only yesterday, before we made them swim with Sobek, the great crocodile god, did they not reveal that the queen, also, is a spy? And now that we know these things, her daughter interrupts this ceremony, this blessing of your glorious war."

"This makes no sense," Arthur shouted. "Why would Nefi and Thami want to start a war?"

"They did not expect a war, snake, as you know.

They expected the mighty pharaoh, their father, to pay tribute to their Nubian relations. The people of Egypt and our great pharaoh WILL NOT LET THAT HAPPEN!"

The crowd recognised their cue, and began roaring their rage for the Nubians and their approval for the high priest, who released Nefi and waved his arms wildly at them, exhorting them to louder and louder fury until the pharaoh turned to the crowd and silenced them with one raised hand.

Where on earth are Finn and the others? Arthur wondered, silently begging them to hurry up and make an appearance.

"We will hear what my daughter has to say," said the pharaoh, turning to her and raising his other hand to pre-empt any protest from the high priest.

"This boy," he said, indicating Arthur. "Who is he and why does he say these things?"

Nefi explained how the two brothers had saved her life that night in Thebes. She told the whole story as truly as she could. From time to time the high priest would make outraged spluttering noises, but he did not interrupt.

"The high priest wants war," Nefi concluded. "He hates the Nubians, as you know, and he wants to see you weakened also. He tricked the Nubian spies into believing that you would pay tribute, knowing that you would not. He let it slip to them that Thamose and I would be in the desert a few days ago, and he made sure that it was temple guards loyal to him who accompanied us on the hunt. He used us as bait. He made it so easy for the Nubians to take Thamose, knowing that it would provoke war. He does not love you, Father; he hates you nearly as much as he hates all Nubians."

The pharaoh was silent for a long while. "The high priest is the messenger of the gods," he said slowly.

"No, Father, YOU are their messenger, just as YOU and not the high priest will one day become a god yourself."

Everyone waited on tenterhooks to hear how the pharaoh would judge, so much so that few other than Arthur noticed the temple guard who walked over to whisper in the high priest's ear. With a sinking feeling of dread, Arthur saw a wicked smile spread across the high priest's face. He murmured a few words to the guard, who disappeared inside the temple.

"Great pharaoh," said the high priest, in a measured tone, "perhaps you will allow me to demonstrate how the Nubian sickness has spread? I am told that less than an hour ago my men apprehended not one but three more Nubian spies. They were asking after the two spies who we got rid of yesterday. BRING THEM FORWARD!"

All heads turned to the temple gateway, through which three hooded figures were driven by the palace guards, one of them was limping heavily. Arthur's heart skipped a beat. The crowd bellowed, loving the spectacle as the high priest began his showmanship once more.

"Behold the face of our enemy!" he cried, whipping off one of the hoods to reveal Finn's bewildered face.

"Behold the face of the desert dog who thinks he may feed from the lion's kill!" he thundered, removing a second hood to reveal Shaharqo's Nubian features.

"Behold the face of those who would grind Thebes INTO THE DUST!" he finished, the crowd booing and jeering now as the final hood was removed to reveal Thami's angry glare.

"Great pharaoh," cried the high priest triumphantly, "your enemies send their spies to the city. They kidnap your children and set your queen against you. The time has come for you to show the world your might. Kill these spies! Kill the queen! And KILL... Thamose?" The high priest nearly choked on the name as he glanced in Thami's direction and finally noticed who he was. There was a noise of wonder from

the crowd. Never had they been so entertained. Thami raised his arm and pointed accusingly at the high priest, who was temporarily speechless.

"The priest, Father. The priest is the sickness in your kingdom. Who commands the men who accompanied Nefru and me on our hunt? The priest! Who in this kingdom hates the Nubians more than any other? The priest! Who found your Nubian spies and interrogated them, Father?"

"The priest," said the pharaoh, slowly.

"And who urged you to lead the army into battle, Father, knowing that you have never fought in battle before?"

"The priest!" repeated the pharaoh as the crowd began to boo and jeer once more.

"Great pharaoh," the high priest beseeched, "this is madness..." But Shaharqo cut him off.

"My name is Shaharqo, Prince of Nubia. I helped to kidnap your son because my general was informed by our spies that they had overheard the high priest discussing your military strengths. He said that you would not be able to muster an army large enough to take them on. He said that the Nubians would be able to exact tribute from you if they knew. These were lies, but he said them to lure my father's armies into provoking a war. Your son and I are here to make peace between our two peoples."

"I have heard enough!" The pharaoh held up his hand once more, and everyone fell silent. "High Priest, this does not look good for you. We will let the crocodile god decide. Guards, bring the priest to the lake of Sobek! Thamose, you and your companions will walk with me."

The pharaoh turned and led the way into the temple, with Thami, Nefi, Arthur, Finn and Shaharqo in a line behind him. The temple guards brought the high priest, who was shouting at them with increasing desperation as he realised that not even they would remain loyal to him after such a public exposure.

They proceeded through the temple courtyard, and through inner chambers covered in intricately painted scenes of men and gods, until they reached an enclosed pool of crystal-clear water.

I wonder where the water is piped from... thought Arthur, and then all thoughts left his mind. Deep down in the clear water, something was moving. It took a few moments for Arthur to realise that it was the swishing tail of a huge crocodile.

The high priest was beginning to jabber now. Gone were the pleas of innocence as he fell on the pharaoh's mercy.

"Put the bridge in place," the pharaoh commanded, ignoring the priest. Two guards brought forward a long, thin beam, no thicker than the width of a man's foot, one end of which they placed on either side of the pool so that it spanned the middle of the water less than a metre above the surface.

"Pray to Sobek for mercy!" the pharaoh growled. The guards dragged the high priest to one end of the beam.

"Great pharaoh, after all we have been through…" But the pharaoh brought his whip down across the priest's shoulders, causing him to howl in pain and take his first, shuddering step onto the beam.

The crocodile began to slant up through the water. The pharaoh brought his whip down again, causing the priest to lurch forwards. The crocodile's head emerged from the water and its transparent eyelid slid open. The priest began to take quick, tiny steps forward, realising that his only hope was to reach the other side.

The reptile dived down lazily and the priest almost collapsed with relief. Too soon. With a sudden surge, the crocodile powered up and thrust the upper part of its body out of the water, huge jaws gaping. Arthur looked away. The priest screamed. The crocodile's jaws snapped closed and there was a loud splash. When Arthur looked back, the priest and the crocodile had disappeared and the churning water had a distinctly reddish hue.

* * *

"There's a sandstorm coming," said Shaharqo, looking up at a starless night sky. "What a day it has been!" All five friends were sitting on the balcony of Thami's room. Following the death of the high priest, events had unfolded rapidly. The pharaoh had announced to the people gathered at the temple that he would send peace envoys to the Nubians. Nefi, Thami and the queen were publicly embraced, which was almost unheard of by all accounts. Shaharqo was told to report to his father, the King of Nubia, that Egypt would be an ally in future. Best of all, the pharaoh had announced that it was time for Thami to begin formal training with the charioteers in the army, leaving Finn and Arthur sure that their work in Egypt was done.

"And we could not have done any of it without our merchant friends," said Thami, putting his arms around Finn and Arthur's shoulders just as the first swirls of dust began to sweep in from the desert.

"We had better go inside," said Nefi. Finn and Arthur looked at one another and smiled. They both knew the adventure was over.

"We'll catch you up," said Arthur, pulling Finn to his feet. They walked over to the edge of the balcony and stared one last time at the temple statues, illuminated by torchlight. The air grew thicker and thicker as the dust particles were replaced by sand that stung their faces. Soon the temple, the palace and even the balcony beneath them were obscured. They felt as if their feet had left the ground and they were spinning through the sandstorm, faster and faster until at last even the sand was no longer there.

BONUS BITS!
Who's Who?

There are lots of characters in the story. Can you match the characters with what they do?

1. Professor Blade

2. Thamose

3. Princess Nefru

4. High Priest

5. Prince Shaharqo

6. Finn

7. Caro

8. Mery

9. Nubian General

a. rescued Finn and Nefi and took them to his house

b. got eaten by a crocodile

c. used to be an archaeologist

d. led the raiding party to capture Thamose

e. was Nefi's Mother's cook

f. claimed to not be a thief

g. wanted to become a charioteer in the army

h. took Thamose and Arthur captive

i. cracked and injured his foot against a hard stone

INTERESTING WORDS
(not covered by Finn's notes)

There is a lot of vocabulary related to the ancient Egyptian world in the story. Here is a short guide to the words that Finn doesn't help you with!

MUMMY
A body of a human being or animal that is preserved (ceremoniously) and wrapped in bandages

NILE DELTA
The delta in northern Egypt where the Nile river spreads out and drains into the Mediterranean Sea

PHARAOH
The title of an ancient Egyptian king

PYRAMID
A structure with a square or triangular base and sloping sides that meet in a point at the top, built of stone in ancient Egypt as royal tombs

SCYTHE
A farming tool with a curved blade and long handle used for cutting grass and crops

SOBEK
An ancient Egyptian god, associated with the Nile crocodile, represented in crocodile form or as a human with a crocodile head

TAVERN
An inn or public house

THEBES
A city known as 'Waset' by the ancient Egyptians, located east of the Nile and with ruins in the modern city of Luxor

WHAT NEXT?

If you enjoyed this story, why not carry out some research to find out what it was like to train as a charioteer (like Thamose is going to do)? When you have done your research using books and/or the internet, write a diary entry pretending to be the person training, to show what a day of training is like.

Answers to 'Who's Who?'

1.	c	6.	i
2.	g	7.	a
3.	f	8.	e
4.	b	9.	h
5.	d		

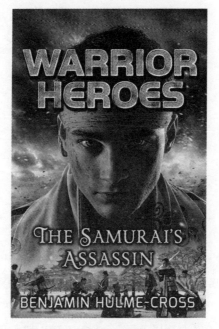

WARRIOR HEROES
The Samurai's Assassin

Benjamin Hulme-Cross

Trapped in their great grandfather's museum
and visited by the restless ghosts of warriors past,
Arthur and Finn must travel back in time and
rewrite history to set the ghosts free. Will the boys
put a stop to the powerful warlord Kenji Kuroda
seizing power once and for all?

£4.99

9781472904669

About the author

Growing up in London, I spent a lot of time sitting on the Underground, daydreaming and reading books. Historical adventures in far-flung lands were always my favourites, and I used to love visiting castles and ruins.

After I left home I lived in Japan for a while and learned all about the Samurai. Now I've swapped the city for the countryside, and as well as reading books I also write stories and plays for young people.

The thing I like most about being a writer is playing around with ideas for stories in my head, which is daydreaming really, so not much has changed!